Don't forget to water the plants.

Do not cut space between arm and body.

Baking a birthday cake!

The movie
is 3D!

Take dainty
little stitches.

My favorite
library book.

Tennis
anyone?

Shopping
is fun!

Strike!

Hello Dear,
It's Grandma
calling!

Let's go
fishing!

GO
FIS

Yum! Ice cream!

Painting
pretty
pictures!

Picnic on
the beach!

I'll help
trim the tree.

Happy
Easter!

Happy Halloween!

Trick or Treat!